Nadia and the Forever Kitten

Nadia and the Forever Kitten

by Holly Webb

Illustrated by Sophy Williams

tiger tales

This book was inspired by my cat Star!

tiger tales

5 River Road, Suite 128, Wilton, CT 06897
Published in the United States 2022
Originally published in Great Britain 2021
by the Little Tiger Group
Text copyright © 2021 Holly Webb
Illustrations copyright © 2021 Sophy Williams
ISBN-13: 978-1-6643-4014-5
ISBN-10: 1-6643-4014-9
Printed in China
STP/1800/0437/1121
10 9 8 7 6 5 4 3 2 1

www.tigertalesbooks.com

Contents

Chapter One
Meeting the Kittens

"I can't believe we'll be in fifth grade next year," Nadia said as she and Violet gathered up the pens and pencils and odd items out of their desks. It was the last day of school before summer vacation, and they had to clean everything up before the final assembly.

"I know!" Violet shook her head.

"We'll be the oldest when we come back in September. Oh, I can't wait for vacation. Are you going away?"

Nadia sighed. "No. Not this summer. My dad gave up his job to start his own business. He has to work really hard, and we can't afford a vacation. Mom said we'll have some fun days out instead, though. Go to New York City for the day, maybe. What about you?"

"I'm going to stay with my dad in August," Violet said. "But my mom's too busy working at the animal rescue center for us to go away. Summer means kitten time. We already have so many to take care of!"

Violet's mom, Michelle, worked for a charity that rescued stray cats, and Violet got to help out during her school breaks. Her mom brought a lot of her work home....

Nadia gave her an envious look. "Lucky!"

"I know." Violet smiled. "They're really cute. Mom's a little worried, though; she says we're running out of space. If more cats show up, we won't have anywhere to put them. We already have kittens in our bathroom."

"That sounds so cool. Can I come and see them?"

"Course you can. Actually, you can have them…. It's really tricky if you get up to go to the bathroom in the middle of the night!"

"Violet!" Nadia giggled.

"It is!" But Violet started laughing, too.

Two days later, Nadia went over to Violet's house to see the kittens. Violet had told her they were just starting to stumble around, like three little furry balloons with legs. They were named Trevor, Tilly, and Tim.

"What happened to their mom?"

Nadia asked. She was sitting on the
bathroom floor with Trevor, a tiny
black kitten, slumped asleep in her lap.

"We don't know," Violet said sadly.
"Mom said they were found in a box
by some garbage cans. Someone heard
them squeaking and brought them to
the rescue. We have to bottle-feed them.
Even in the middle of the night!"

Nadia sighed at the thought. The
kittens were so beautiful—she wouldn't
mind waking up to do that. She ran
her finger over Trevor's dusty black fur,
and he shivered and twitched in his
sleep.

"You can help feed them now," Violet
suggested. "They're going to wake up
starving any second." Almost as soon
as she had said it, Tim, the black-

and-white kitten draped over her leg, opened his dark blue eyes and started to make bossy little squeaking noises.

"Are you sure?" Nadia said eagerly. "I don't want to get it wrong."

Violet grinned. "They won't let you. They're little milk-monsters. You just hold the bottle and watch them go."

Violet was right. As soon as the kittens saw Violet's mom arrive with their bottles, there was no stopping them. They erupted into even more pleading squeaks, begging to go first.

"Oh, you're so greedy," Violet's mom said, laughing as Tilly pawed at her legs, trying to reach the bottle. "It's okay; there's enough for everyone." She handed a bottle to Nadia. "Do you want to feed Trevor?"

Nadia nodded and then giggled as three kittens suddenly surged toward her. She held the bottle up to Trevor's mouth, and the kitten lunged at it. She laughed as he made slurping noises around the rubber teat.

After he finished, Trevor stretched out along Nadia's jeans, purring in a very smug, satisfied way.

"He's so handsome," Nadia sighed. "But isn't it hard, spending all of this time with them and then having to give them to someone else?" Violet had already explained that they only kept the kittens while they needed around-the-clock care—then they went back to the rescue to be adopted into their forever homes.

Violet tickled Tim behind the ears and looked thoughtful. "I guess I'm used to it. I mean, of course it's sad to say good-bye, but then I think of them having loving homes, where they're bossing everyone around and being super spoiled."

Her mother laughed. "The new owners send me photos sometimes. It's really nice to see the kittens I knew as big, grown-up cats."

Violet nodded. "She puts them up around the rescue center, and it makes me feel so proud. It's like—we were part of that!"

"It would be special…," Nadia agreed, looking thoughtful. She imagined how good it would feel to help a kitten like Trevor find a forever home.

Violet nudged her. "If you're going to be home all summer, you could take care of some kittens, you know. At your house. You're always looking for people to foster, aren't you, Mom?"

"Always." Violet's mom sighed. "I didn't tell you, but I got a call this morning from an elderly lady who found a feral cat in her yard. She thinks the cat is pregnant. I'm going over tomorrow to see if I can catch her." The doorbell rang, and Violet's mom got up. "That's probably your mom, Nadia. I'll go and let her in."

"Do you think your mom and dad would let you?" Violet whispered as her mom headed downstairs.

"I don't know…. I've always wanted a cat, and maybe now that Dad is going to be working from home…." Nadia gave Violet a hopeful look. "It's worth a try!"

There was a gentle knock at the bathroom door. "Do you have all of those kittens safe?" Violet's mom called.

"Yes!" Violet said.

Her mom opened the door carefully, explaining to Nadia's mom, "They're getting so adventurous now. They shoot out of the door so fast, and I don't want them falling down the stairs!"

Nadia waved at her mom, who was

standing behind Violet's mom and
looking curious.

"Mom, this is Trevor. Isn't he
beautiful?"

"Oh, he is very sweet," her mom
said, leaning down to look at the kitten
climbing Nadia's T-shirt. She smiled at
Violet's mom. "I can't believe you have
a bathroom full of kittens!"

Michelle sighed. "Tell me about it. We don't have staff at the rescue center during the night, and these little ones need feeding at all hours, so we try to foster them out. We're running out of people to foster, though. There are so many kittens being born right now—and it's summer vacation, so a lot of our foster families are going away."

"Mom…," Nadia started to say, and her mom laughed.

"I bet I know what you're going to ask!" she said.

"Well, couldn't we?" Nadia pleaded. "It was so much fun feeding Trevor."

"I'm not sure you'd think it was fun in the middle of the night," her mom said gently. "Your dad may be at home, Nadia, but I still have to get up and go to work. I'm not sure I can cope with kitten feedings at three in the morning, or whenever!" She smiled apologetically at Violet's mom. "Though they are beautiful…. Hello, sweetheart…." She was talking to Tilly, who was investigating the laces on her sneakers. She crouched down to tickle her under the chin and then laughed when Tilly erupted in a wild purr.

"I know what you mean about nighttime feedings," Violet's mom said, shuddering. "It's exhausting. And don't worry. I'm not about to send you home with kittens! Although…." She paused, looking thoughtfully at Nadia's mom. "It isn't only orphaned kittens we take care of. We do have older cats who need fostering sometimes. I was just telling the girls I received a call about a pregnant stray this morning. She needs a quiet place with no other cats around for giving birth. And when the kittens are born, she'll feed them herself. Worth considering, if you did want to help out. Just give me a call if you'd like to try."

Nadia fixed her mom with a hopeful stare. A mother cat and the tiniest possible kittens, in their house! "We're not going away," she reminded her. "I wouldn't mind if we didn't go on day trips." "It's definitely something to think about," her mom said slowly. "But we'll have to talk to your dad first. He's the one who's going to be at home most of the time with you and a cat."

"And adorable kittens," Nadia added.

"Yes, and very sweet kittens," her mom agreed, laughing at Tilly, who was on her back fighting a battle with a shoelace. "I promise we'll think about it, Nadia. We'll think about it."

Chapter Two
Welcoming Gracie

Nadia tried so hard not to pester Mom about Violet's mom's idea on the way home, but she couldn't get it out of her head.

"You're very quiet," her mom said as they walked along their street.

Nadia looked up and her mom was smiling. She must have figured out exactly what Nadia was thinking.

"I didn't want to go on about it, Mom," she said. "But I can't think of anything else!" She couldn't stop herself from bouncing a little bit as she walked. "Just think! A cat! In our house! And kittens!"

"But not a cat we can keep," her mom pointed out. "It would only be for a while, Nadia. Wouldn't you miss her when she's gone? And the kittens? I think it might be hard to say good-bye."

Nadia nodded. "I asked Violet about that. She said she's used to it, and it would be harder for us. But knowing that we'll be helping the kittens find forever homes would make it easier. And Violet's mom says they really do need the help. I think that would make it worth being sad when we say good-bye. Don't you?"

Mom nodded, and Nadia thought
she looked a little surprised. "Yes...."
She leaned down and put her arm
around Nadia's shoulders for a quick
hug. "I love that you're so thoughtful."

Nadia crossed her fingers behind her
back, feeling hopeful. But what was
her dad going to say?

Afterward, Nadia wondered if it was
down to how cute Tilly had been,
playing with Mom's shoelaces. Or
maybe it was because Dad was feeling
happy about a good day at work.
Whatever the reason, her mom called
Violet's mom later that evening to say

yes, they would foster the pregnant cat—the elderly lady had named her Gracie. Violet's mom was going to pick her up in the morning and take her for a checkup at the vet.

The following day, Nadia got up early and put away all of the dishes that had been left on the draining board overnight. Then she plugged in the vacuum cleaner and started cleaning the living room. When her mom came downstairs, she looked confused.

"Nadia, what are you doing?"

Nadia glanced around. "I'm cleaning up for Gracie."

"I don't think she's going to notice if the carpet's dusty…." Her mom smiled. "But it's very nice of you. I'll go make some toast."

By eleven, when Violet's mom was due to arrive with Gracie, Nadia was in the middle of cleaning her bedroom. She wanted everything to be perfect—*and* she was too excited to sit still. When the doorbell rang, she raced down the stairs in three jumps. She forced herself not to fling the front door wide open—Violet's mom had told Mom on the phone that Gracie would be really nervous because she was a feral cat, and she was about to have kittens. They would have to be quiet and gentle around her.

"Hi!" she whispered to Violet's mom, and she beamed at Violet, who was standing beside her mom with a soft cat bed, a bag of food, and all kinds of other things in her arms. Violet's mom was carrying a plastic box with a wire front, and Nadia could see a furry face looking back at her from inside.

"Hi, Michelle, hello, Violet!" Nadia's mom hurried out from the kitchen, and her dad came down from his office. "Come on in. Should we take her upstairs? We were going to put her in the spare room."

"That sounds great," Violet's mom said, and they all followed Nadia's dad upstairs. Violet's mom carefully put the carrier down on the floor. "Hopefully we've brought everything you'll need."

"There's so much," Nadia muttered. She was carrying some of Violet's big pile now—food bowls and a bag of cat litter, and what looked like a couple of cat toys.

"Can we fill up the litter box and her water bowl, maybe offer her a little dry food to cheer her up?" Violet's mom suggested. "Then we'll see if she wants to come out. It might take a while; she's very shy. She's been living in an elderly lady's yard until now—apparently she let Mrs. Jackson pet her occasionally, but she never came into the house."

Nadia looked up from filling the litter box, eyeing the cat carrier hopefully. It sounded as though Gracie might be almost friendly, if she didn't mind being petted.

Violet's mom unlatched the wire door of the carrier and stepped back. "Hey, Gracie," she said gently. "Want to come and see your new place?"

There was a rustle inside the carrier, and then a nose appeared at the wire door, followed by some whiskers.

Nadia guessed that Gracie was sniffing the air, trying to figure out where she'd ended up. It must all seem very strange to her.

No sooner than they'd appeared, the whisker-tips shrank back inside the carrier, and Violet's mom sighed. "Don't worry. I think Gracie just needs time to get used to the idea. I'm sure she'll come out soon. Thanks so much for preparing a room for her—this is perfect."

Nadia's mom and dad led Violet and her mom downstairs for a cup of tea, but Nadia couldn't help lingering as her mom closed the door, peering around for one last look.

Usually during school vacations, Nadia
went to a vacation club, at least for
some of the time, but now that Dad was
working from home, she didn't have to.
She was enjoying being able to sleep in
a little later. It made Monday mornings
a lot nicer. She stretched lazily, yawned,
and rolled over to see what time it was.
It definitely felt like breakfast time.
She would take a quick look around the
door of Gracie's room, too, on the way
downstairs.

But as Nadia reached for her alarm
clock, she froze, staring at the open
closet in the corner of her room.

There, lying on
her shoes, was a
small striped cat,
glaring back at her.

Nadia swallowed. "Um…. You're not supposed to be there," she whispered to Gracie. "You have your own room…." She was almost sure Gracie was scowling, but maybe it was just the black M-shape of stripes above her eyes. Nadia slipped out of bed and scurried downstairs to find her mom and dad.

"Gracie's in my closet!" she squeaked to her mom, who was making a cup of tea before she went to work.

"What?" Mom stared at her. "How? She was in the spare room!"

"Not anymore." Nadia shook her head. "I just woke up, and there she was, staring at me!"

Dad looked guilty. "I fed her when I got up…. Maybe I didn't shut the door all the way."

They all hurried back upstairs to look at Gracie, who was still snuggled comfortably among Nadia's things.

"She looks so happy there," Dad said.

"Violet's mom said that when the kittens were close to coming, she'd want to make nests," Nadia remembered. "That's why they brought those fleece blankets. Maybe she's about to have her kittens! Do you think she's nesting in my closet?"

"Maybe," Mom said. "But I don't know if we should let her!"

"I can shut my bedroom door so she doesn't go into the rest of the house," Nadia suggested. "She can't mind my being in here, since she came in while I was asleep!" She smiled at Gracie, and

Gracie glared back, and then yawned and stretched. Her tummy was looking very round, Nadia thought. Soon there would be kittens in her bedroom!

Later that week, Nadia and her mom were at Nadia's nani's house. Nani loved cats, and Nadia was desperate to tell her all about Gracie.

"So do you know when the kittens are coming?" Nani asked hopefully.

"Soon, we think," Mom said.

Nadia sighed. "I was hoping she'd have had them by now. She made her nest in my closet on Monday, and now it's Thursday. Violet's mom said she thought Gracie was due any day!"

Nani chuckled. "Maybe she likes keeping you guessing. She obviously has a mind of her own."

"I think you're right," Mom agreed. "Actually, we should get back to check on her now, Nadia. Dad went out for a meeting, so Gracie's been on her own for a couple of hours. We'll see you soon, Mama."

Nadia gave Nani a hug. "We'll call

and tell you when she has the kittens," she promised. "You can come and see them!"

"I'd love that," Nani said. "I still miss my Milo...."

"Aw, Nani." Nadia hugged her again harder. She'd loved fussing over Nani's cat Milo when they visited. He had been a huge, white, long-haired cat, definitely the biggest cat Nadia had ever seen. He had been three times the size of Gracie. "Me, too. He was so friendly. I'd better go. See you soon!"

As they walked home, Nadia began to worry. "Do you think there might be something wrong with Gracie?" she asked her mom. "Maybe we should take her to the vet."

Mom frowned. "Violet's mom told

us they didn't know exactly when Gracie was due. Just soon. I'm sure it's okay, Nadia."

"I guess." Nadia sighed. But it seemed like they'd already waited so long. She was desperate to meet Gracie's kittens.

Dad was just returning from his meeting when they got home, so Nadia hurried upstairs to check on Gracie while her mom and dad chatted in the kitchen. The tabby cat was definitely friendlier than she had been when she first arrived. She still looked a little suspicious whenever Nadia walked in (which Nadia thought was a little unfair, really, since it was her bedroom), but then she seemed to relax. She didn't mind if Nadia sat close by on her beanbag and read a book, or lay on the floor and drew. Nadia had drawn a lot of cats....

Nadia opened the door quietly, still trying hard not to scare Gracie. "Hey," she whispered as she tiptoed in. "My nani's really excited about you—Oh! Gracie!" Nadia stopped in the middle of her bedroom, gazing wide-eyed at her closet.

Gracie was stretched out on her side, and next to her were five tiny bundles of fur.

Chapter Three
The Tiniest Kitten

Nadia closed the door very quietly and stood on the other side of it for a moment, her eyes huge and round, her heart thumping. Her closet was full of kittens! Then she raced to find her parents.

"Mom! Dad! She had them! Gracie had the kittens while we were at Nani's!" she yelled from halfway down the stairs, and her mom and dad both came out into the hallway looking shocked.

"Is she okay?" Dad asked.

"I didn't look for very long," Nadia admitted. "I was so surprised, so I just came to tell you. But I think so. They were all lying next to her. I think they were feeding."

"We were supposed to call Violet's mom when Gracie started giving birth!" Mom said, her face worried. "Let's take a quick look, and then I'll give her a call."

They padded softly back up the stairs, whispery and excited, and peered around Nadia's door. Gracie lifted her head wearily to watch them, but she didn't seem too bothered that they were there.

"They look okay, don't they?" Nadia whispered. "I love the way they're lined up!" The kittens were all feeding, lying next to each other in a neat little row.

"They're so different," Mom said.

Nadia nodded. She had assumed that all of the kittens would look just like Gracie, but although there were two perfect tabbies, there were also two soft, smoky-gray kittens and one tiny orange one, with long white boots and a white front. Nadia hadn't really been ready for how small the kittens would be, either—like furry beanbags, with stubby pink paws poking out. Their eyes were closed, and they nuzzled and squeaked and squirmed up against Gracie.

"Can I stay in here?" Nadia asked quietly. "I just want to look at the kittens for a while. Do you think Gracie will mind?"

Nadia's mom put her hand over her mouth to muffle a laugh. "I think she might be too tired to care, Nadia. I'll call Violet's mom. She'll want to come over and make sure they're all healthy."

"I'll stay and watch with you," Dad said, sitting on the end of Nadia's bed so he could see inside the closet. "I've never seen such tiny kittens. And she managed it all by herself, without us even knowing about it. You're amazing, Gracie…."

The smallest of the kittens stretched
out her paws blindly, squeaking
for milk. She was so hungry. She
twisted her head around, trying to
find somewhere to suck. One of the
big gray kittens blundered into her,
accidentally pushing her out of the
way—he was hungry, too, and he didn't
even notice that he'd shoved his little
sister.

The little orange kitten meowed
and wriggled, sniffing the air for the
smell of milk. She waved her paws,
still squeaking for attention, and then
her mother nudged her close, nuzzling
her up against the other kittens. The
orange kitten squeaked again, catching
the scent of milk, and latched on at last.
But she was so tired, and it was hard
work suckling. She drank a little and
dozed, and then drank a little more.

The big gray kitten scrambled closer,
eager for milk, and bumped his tiny
sister again. She gave a faint meow of
surprise, and then she curled herself
away from his nudging paws and
drifted back to sleep....

When her mom and dad agreed to take care of Gracie, Nadia had never dreamed that she'd end up with five kittens in her bedroom—but she wasn't complaining, even though the kittens' little squeaks and mumbles often woke her up in the night. Even Violet had never had a bedroom full of kittens, and she was jealous when she finally got to meet them a few days later.

"You have kittens in your bathroom!" Nadia pointed out.

"And the kitchen now, too." Violet sighed. "Mom said she couldn't turn the last bunch away. There are kittens *everywhere*. But I'd love to have them in my bedroom. Yours are so sweet, especially the plushy gray ones."

The gray kittens were beautiful, but

Nadia thought the tiny orange one was the sweetest. She always seemed to be at the bottom of the kitten pile, being stomped on by her brothers and sisters. She was much smaller than the others, too.

Nadia and her mom and dad had been talking about names for the kittens—Nadia had decided that Luna suited the orange kitten. The white patch under her chin was almost a perfect circle, like a full moon. Mom wanted to call the two gray kittens Jo and Jem, and the tabbies were Ani and Arya.

"I wonder what color their eyes will be," Nadia said, smiling as Jo—or at least she thought it was Jo—scrambled over the pile of kittens and slumped onto Gracie's back for a nap. Gracie looked a little surprised.

"They won't open for about a week, but they'll all have blue eyes to start with," Violet said. "Then they'll change when they're a couple of weeks old."

"I never knew that!"

"Their ears are closed up when they're born, too," Violet told her. "They're probably only starting to hear now."

Just then, Violet's mom came in with Nadia's parents—they'd been having a cup of tea downstairs. She kneeled on the floor a little way from the closet and looked thoughtfully at Gracie and the kittens. "She looks very proud of herself," she said, smiling.

"Do you think the kittens are okay?" Nadia asked anxiously.

"They look fine." Violet's mom leaned a little closer, trying not to upset Gracie. Then she glanced back at Nadia. "Why? Are you worried about them?"

Nadia shrugged. Violet's mom knew so much about cats, and so did Violet. She didn't want to say something silly. But she *was* worried.... "It's just ... the little orange one. She's smaller than the others, and I don't think she's getting as much milk as they are. It's like she's too sleepy to bother feeding for long." She smiled shyly at Violet's mom. "I've been watching them a lot."

Violet's mom nodded. "That's really useful to know, Nadia. Good job! She's definitely looking a little small, and she's not moving around as much as the other kittens, either."

48

Nadia didn't know whether to be happy or not. She was glad she'd been right, but she didn't want Luna to have something wrong with her. "Will she be okay?" she asked, crouching down next to Violet's mom. Luna was curled up on her own, a little way off from the other kittens.

"I think she just needs more food," Violet's mom said thoughtfully.

"Gracie has tried to get her to feed," Nadia said. "I saw her picking Luna up in her mouth! She was trying to get

49

her closer. But the other kittens have started wriggling around now, and they squish her...."

Violet's mom nodded. "I know. They don't mean to, but it's easy for the weakest kitten to get pushed out. I think Luna—is that what you're calling her? I think she might need some help." She smiled at Nadia. "Remember how good you were at feeding Trevor?"

"Oh!" Nadia reached out excitedly to grab Violet's hand and squeeze it. "But... Luna's so little. Although I guess Trevor and Tilly and Tim were that size, too, when you started."

"Exactly." Violet's mom looked at Nadia's mom and dad. "Do you think you'll be able to do it? It looks like Luna's still getting some milk from

Gracie, so we just need to top her off. But it will mean feeding her every couple of hours—although you can probably get away with every four hours during the night."

Nadia's dad looked worriedly at her mom.

"It's a lot, I know," Violet's mom said. "I can try to find a more experienced foster home if this is going to be too much. I did say Gracie would feed the kittens herself!"

There was silence for a moment, and Nadia glanced anxiously from her mom to her dad. Every two hours was a lot to ask.

"Well … it's your bedroom, Nadia," Dad said slowly. "I'm guessing Gracie won't want us to move her back to the spare room."

"I don't mind!" Nadia said quickly.

"I honestly can't imagine sending them somewhere else." Dad shrugged. "I've gotten used to popping in to check on them every time I take a break from working for a cup of tea. Gracie's such a good mom— she just needs a little help with Luna. She's a lot less jumpy, too. I think she's starting to trust us."

Mom laughed. "I was expecting it to be Nadia who fell in love with them, not you!"

Dad put his arm around Nadia. "Me and Nadia both, I think."

52

Chapter Four
Getting Bigger

"Your eyes are opening!"

Luna blinked sleepily up at the voice above her. She knew that voice, the softer, lighter one. The girl, the one who fed her.

"They're blue, just like Violet said they would be," Nadia whispered as she gently rubbed Luna's head. "This is so exciting, Luna. You can see me! At

least, you'll be able to soon. I suppose
you don't really understand what's
happening right now."

Luna wriggled and let out a tiny,
wailing squeak, hoping for milk.
Where was the bottle? She could
smell milk…. She tried to focus on the
girl, on Nadia, leaning over her, but
all she could really see were shapes
and shadows. She padded her paws
frantically against the soft cat bed,
blundering toward Nadia, and food.

"It's okay, here you go. Look…."
Luna felt herself lifted gently onto
a soft towel and then the teat of the
bottle brushed against her mouth. She
sucked at it eagerly, spluttering milk all
around her face to start with and then
settling in to a slow, steady gulp.

"You're getting so good at this now. I'm sure I can see you growing, Luna…. There, you've almost finished it."

Luna slurped happily at the last few drops in the bottle and then slumped back onto the towel in a milky daze. She shivered a little as Nadia gently wiped her face and then ran her finger along her back. She let out a tiny purr, arching into the soft fingers, and she heard Nadia laugh. Then Luna felt herself lifted again, cupped carefully in Nadia's hands, and then laid down alongside her mother.

She twitched her ears as Gracie began to lick her clean and snuggled in closer to the softly breathing pile of kittens.

"Oh, Nadia. They're getting so big! Are you still bottle-feeding the little orange one?" Nani sat down on the edge of Nadia's bed and peered admiringly at the kittens.

"Yes, but we won't have to for much longer, Violet's mom said. They're three weeks old, so we can start giving them kitten food soon. We have to mix it with milk—it's going to be so messy."

"That's good. You wouldn't want to be up during the night feeding her once you're back at school."

56

Nadia made a face. "It's a while before I go back to school, though. We're only halfway through summer vacation." Halfway.... She couldn't imagine going back to school and not spending all day with Gracie and the kittens.

"You've done so well feeding her," Nani said. "I called her the little one, but she's almost as big as the others now."

"She is," Nadia said proudly. She looked down at Luna, who was curled comfortably in her lap, and smiled. Luna's orange fur was looking thick and fluffy, and her white boots shone—all those bottles of milk were working. "She's not quite as brave as the others, though. They love exploring my bedroom, and they get everywhere."

"I can see," Nani said, laughing as Jo started to climb up her pants.

"Ooooh! I'm glad I have churidar on, Nadia, because she's digging her claws in!"

Nadia gently unhooked the gray kitten and popped her back into the cat bed next to Gracie. "She won't be there for long," she said, shaking her head. "She's the most adventurous of them all."

Jo might be the bravest, but Nadia thought that Luna was the sweetest of the kittens—maybe it was because she'd been hand-feeding her, and it made her seem special. But Luna did seem to love her back. She always wobbled over to Nadia whenever Nadia came into the room. She'd sit on her hind paws, batting at Nadia's legs and asking to be picked up. She always wanted to sleep on Nadia, too— sometimes when she was really tired, Luna would just collapse on Nadia's feet, as if she didn't have the energy to climb any higher. Even in the hot summer weather, Nadia thought there was nothing nicer than a tiny kitten slumped asleep on her foot.

Even though Nadia had been sure the summer would last forever, the second half of vacation seemed to fly by even faster than the first. All too soon, Nadia's dad was telling her to make sure her school bag was ready, and asking if she needed him to get her any more white socks.

The kittens were six weeks old now and eating solid food, although they still fed from Gracie, too. Luna didn't really need Nadia to bottle-feed her any more, but she was still having one bottle a day—mostly because if she didn't get it, she would squeak and complain like anything, and Nadia just couldn't resist. Violet's mom had said it wouldn't do her any harm and that Luna would grow out of milk soon anyway.

Now that the kittens were getting so much bigger, Violet's mom and the staff at the rescue center were starting to think about new homes for them. The kittens had already been featured on the rescue's website as being available soon. Nadia didn't know whether to be happy or sad. She was so proud of her kittens, going off to forever homes—but she hated the thought of saying good-bye.

"I've gotten quite a few messages about the kittens," Violet's mom told Nadia and her dad when they met at the school gates on the first morning back. "Especially the two gray ones. The tabbies, too."

"Not little Luna?" Dad asked, sounding surprised.

"Not as much as the others," Violet's mom admitted.

Nadia frowned. Why wouldn't anyone want Luna?

"So would it be all right if a couple of people came to see them over the next week?" Violet's mom asked. "To see if they'd like to adopt one, once they're ready to leave Gracie?"

"I can't imagine them leaving her," Nadia said. "Gracie takes care of them all so well. Especially Luna. It feels like she needs her mom…."

Violet's mom smiled. "Gracie's a very good mother. But she needs time to herself now, too—we want her to start getting used to being away from the kittens so that she's ready for them to leave, too. Maybe you could let her explore a different room."

Dad brightened. "She can be in my office. I'd like the company, actually. She's much friendlier than she was when she first arrived."

Nadia chewed her bottom lip. Dad was right—Gracie seemed to enjoy being petted now, as long as they picked the right moment. It seemed sad that she had to get used to being separated from her kittens, but maybe she'd like the peace and quiet. Nadia still didn't want to think about the kittens leaving her and Gracie behind.

"Oh, they're so sweet!"

Luna woke up with a start. She'd been snoozing, snuggled up against her mother, but now there was someone strange and loud in the room. Luna was used to Nadia, and her mom—and dad, and even Nani and Violet and her mom, but this was someone different. She retreated behind Gracie, who was sitting up now, eyeing the visitor suspiciously.

"So the two tabby kittens are girls, the gray ones are a girl and a boy, and the orange one—we call her Luna—is a girl," Nadia's dad explained.

"I love the gray ones!" the woman exclaimed, crouching down next to the playpen that Nadia's dad had fixed across the front of the closet. Now that

Nadia was back at school, they didn't
want the kittens roaming around her
bedroom, in case they hurt themselves
or got trapped somewhere. Luna didn't
mind the pen, but Jo spent most of her
time trying to mountaineer out of it.
She was getting very good at climbing
the mesh sides, and she was halfway up
there now.

"The orange one looks a little shy,
doesn't she? Is it okay if I pick this
beautiful gray one up?" the woman
asked, and Luna flinched farther back
as she leaned right over the pen and
reached for Jo.

From behind her mother, Luna
watched Jo clambering across the
woman's lap, sniffing and nuzzling at
her. She didn't seem to be frightened

of her at all, not even when the woman laughed, a high, loud noise that made Luna's ears flatten. Her sisters were crowded curiously at the front of the pen, watching the woman cuddle Jo. They patted the mesh with their paws and meowed for their turn to be taken out, to explore, to be petted. Luna just wished Nadia were there.

Over the next few days, the same thing happened again and again. People came, strange people who wanted to fuss over the kittens and pick them up and cuddle them. No one seemed to want to lift Luna out of the pen, but she didn't mind. She was quite happy hidden away at the back. Happy and safe.

Chapter Five
Finding Homes

Violet tickled Arya the tabby kitten under her chin and laughed as she stuck her nose in the air and closed her eyes blissfully. Violet had come home with Nadia after school, and the two girls were sitting on Nadia's bedroom floor with Arya and Luna climbing all over them. "So she's going tomorrow?" Violet asked.

"Yes…." Nadia rubbed Arya's ears, and she began to purr at the double love she was getting. "Then we'll only have Luna left." She made a face. Arya, Ani, Jo, and Jem were all going to perfect forever homes. It seemed so unfair that Luna was left behind. "I don't understand people. I really don't. No one wanted to look at her! Just because she's a little shy. She'd have gone to them if they hadn't been all loud and grabby."

Luna was curled up in Nadia's lap in a tiny orange ball. She kept getting up and looking around, though, as if she just couldn't get comfortable. Nadia wasn't sure if she was worried about the other kittens, or she was looking for Gracie.

The kittens' mother was with Dad in his office—probably stretched out comfortably next to his computer keyboard, which seemed to be her new favorite place. Since Violet's mom had suggested it a couple of weeks ago, Gracie had been having time away from her kittens, but Nadia was sure Luna didn't like it.

"She'll find a home soon," Violet said. She was trying to be reassuring, but Nadia ducked her head, not wanting her friend to see her worried face. "I know she's shy, but someone's going to love her," Violet went on. "And a lot of people really like orange fur."

"Like me!" Nadia said, looking up indignantly. "How could anyone not like orange fur? Luna's gorgeous! I love her white boots. And she has the nicest little pink feet."

Violet laughed. "I know. I think she's beautiful, too."

"You're a lovely color," Nadia whispered comfortingly to Luna. "The prettiest of all the kittens, and don't let anyone tell you different."

Luna peered uncertainly around the edge of Nadia's bedroom door into the hallway. Nadia had left for school a while ago, and the house was quiet.

Even though Luna was starting to get used to Nadia being away during the day, she still missed her, and she was a little bored without the other kittens to play with.

Gracie was curled up on the bed, dozing. Luna had learned how to climb up the edge of the comforter and scramble her way onto the bed, but she didn't feel like snuggling up with her mom. The bedroom door was open, and Luna was feeling adventurous. She was growing up and getting bolder, and now that Nadia's dad had taken the pen away from the closet, she wanted to explore her home.

Luna put her nose through the gap and then glanced back at Gracie on the bed. Her mother had one eye open,

watching her. But that's all she was
doing, just watching. It was all right
then, Luna thought. She was allowed.

More confidently now, she padded
out onto the landing and looked
around. Then a little farther…. Luna
turned to make sure the door was still
there, and it was. She knew how to
get back. Slowly, she walked along
the landing, sniffing and nosing at
the carpet,
the cracks
under the
doors,
a laundry
basket—she
scratched her
paws at that curiously, but she
didn't know what it was.

73

The other doors on the landing were shut, so she stood at the top of the stairs instead, staring down. They were so big! Gracie went down there sometimes, but Luna was sure she could never manage all those steps. She would have to wait for Nadia to carry her, she thought, then she could explore more. Luna slumped down with her chin on the carpet, her paws dangling over the top step, settling into a comfortable doze.

"Is Luna missing the other kittens?" Violet asked. She and Nadia were curled up on one of the playground benches, keeping an eye on a wild game of soccer that was getting close.

"Maybe a little," Nadia said thoughtfully. "She's doing a lot of exploring around the house. And she definitely wants me to play with her more." She smiled, remembering the tiny orange kitten she'd found waiting for her at the top of the stairs the day before. "I love it. She's so funny, and she plays with everything—even my hair!" She twitched the wavy end of her ponytail at Violet. "Gracie's almost started playing, too," she added, looking proud. "Dad said she keeps stealing his pens and knocking them off the table on purpose. And then she stares at him until he picks them up so she can do it all over again!"

"Does he do it?" Violet asked.

"Every time! He really loves having her. I never expected him to like fostering so much. And the more Gracie gets used to living with a family, the more likely she is to be adopted. Don't you think?"

Violet nodded. "Once Luna's been adopted, Gracie can go back to the rescue center. She's a lot less wild than she was, and she's beautiful. It might take a while for her to find a home, because she's so shy…. But I'm sure someone's going to love her." The girls got up as the whistle blew and wandered across the playground to the door.

Nadia was sure that Violet was right, but all afternoon she kept thinking about Gracie and Luna, and finding them their forever homes. *We're doing a good job*, she told herself as she tried to listen to Miss Evans explaining their history project. *I really want Gracie and Luna to go to nice people. I've been worrying for so long that no one wants Luna! And I know that when they do, it'll be because we took care of them so well.* But she couldn't help thinking, *Won't Luna miss me when she goes to live somewhere else? I know I miss her, even when I'm at school. I can't imagine never seeing her again....*

Nadia chewed on the end of her pencil, forgetting about school entirely.

Maybe—maybe we could just keep her. And Gracie. Then they wouldn't have to be split up!

Nadia couldn't understand why she hadn't thought of it before, because now it seemed perfect. Except—they were only supposed to be fostering.... Mom and Dad had never agreed to adopt a cat forever, certainly not a cat *and* a kitten. Nadia heaved a sigh that sent her worksheet halfway across the table and then hurriedly snatched it back, looking embarrassed.

"Are you all right, Nadia?" Miss Evans asked. "Are you stuck?"

"Um.... No," Nadia said, staring down at her blank worksheet. "I'm all right. Sorry." She gritted her teeth and glared at the questions. There was only a tiny bit of the afternoon left, and Mom was picking her up today. Maybe she could talk to her about adopting Gracie and Luna on the way home.

But as she dashed out onto the playground with Violet after school, she saw her mom and Violet's mom standing together in the crowd of parents. They didn't notice as she and Violet arrived, and Nadia saw Violet's mom pat her mom's arm.

"You don't know how grateful we are, Farida. We were really stuck, and it's been so helpful having you take care of Gracie and the kittens."

"We've loved it," Nadia's mom said, smiling. "I was a little doubtful at first, but it's been so special, and it's so nice to see them all going off to their new homes. We'd definitely do it again."

Violet's mom nodded eagerly. "Well, that won't be a problem—we always have cats that need a loving foster home."

Nadia slowed to a walk, biting her lip.

How could she ask her mom to stop fostering when there were so many other cats who needed their help?

Chapter Six
The Discovery

The next day, Luna peered up at her mother, who was stretched out along the desk above her. Every so often, Nadia's dad would stop typing and pet her. If he didn't pet her often enough, Gracie would roll over and tap his arm with her paw. She had him very well trained.

Dad didn't like Luna walking all

around on his keyboard, though. She'd only been trying to follow his fingers, but he'd put her back down on the floor. Luna patted at a pile of books and papers instead, enjoying the rustling noises they made. But it wasn't enough to keep her occupied for long. If Nadia were there, she would have crumpled the paper into a ball and thrown it around for her to chase, Luna thought. Nadia was very good at that, and Luna loved growling fiercely at the scrunched-up paper and then shredding it into pieces with her tiny claws.

Nadia wasn't going to be back for a while, though, Luna was fairly sure. She'd have to find something else to keep her busy. She padded across the carpet and out onto the landing—she was planning to go back to Nadia's room; it was more interesting than Dad's office, and she still wasn't sure about trying to climb down the stairs. Nadia's room had more things to chase and burrow under and play with—the office was too neat and clean.

But suddenly Luna pulled up short, her eyes wide and curious. There was another door, at the end of the landing. She'd seen the door before, of course, but she'd never seen it standing open, the way it was now. There was a faint, fresh smell floating out and a fascinating sound of birdsong. Luna hurried along the landing to investigate and popped her head around the door.

Stretching up in front of her was a
flight of stairs, and Luna eyed them
sadly. Stairs, again! Why
were there always stairs
to stop her? She padded
at the first step with one
paw, catching the carpet
fibers in her claws. The
carpet was easy to grab
on to, she noticed in
surprise. Almost easier
than Nadia's comforter.
If she could climb up
onto Nadia's bed, maybe
she could climb these
steps…. Luna stood up on her back
paws and realized she could actually
reach almost to the top of the step. If
she jumped a little…. She dropped

back, and then leaped and scrambled mightily, finally landing on the first step with a triumphant twitch of her tail.

There were an awful lot more of those steps, though. Luna gazed upward for a moment and then, determined, set about climbing again. She wanted to know what that scent was, and she could feel a breeze ruffling her fur. On and on she clambered, until at last she slumped down on the very top step. She was almost too worn out to realize that she had done it.

But the room was too interesting for Luna to be tired for long. She padded slowly across the floor, looking around at the furniture—particularly the bed, which had all kinds of interesting boxes and bags and shadowy spaces underneath. Luna poked her nose in and then backed out quickly, sneezing at the dust.

She was still shaking her whiskers when she noticed a quiet buzzing over on the other side of the room. Intrigued, Luna hurried around the bed to look. Up above in the sloping ceiling was a window—a strange, angled window that tipped open to show a deep, calm blue sky. And crawling and bumbling around the bottom of the window was a fat, furry bee.

Luna was entranced. She had never seen a bumblebee before. She and Gracie had always been inside the house, and Nadia and Dad had been

very careful not to open their windows,
in case Luna or Gracie climbed out.

It was an effort after her hard climb
up the stairs, but Luna scrambled up
onto the bed to get closer to the frantic
bee. It couldn't seem to figure out how
to get out of the gap again, and it kept
bumping into the glass.

All of Luna's hunting instincts were roused now. She was desperate to get closer. She perched on the very edge of the bed, her bottom wiggling as she measured the jump to the shelving unit under the window. If she could make it there, she would be so close! Just as she sprang, the bee finally figured out what it was doing wrong and zoomed joyfully out into the sky. Luna landed on the top shelf of the unit a second later, slipping and scrambling a little, but safe. Except there was no bee. She peered after it, feeling grumpy. All that hard work, climbing and jumping, and the furry buzzy thing was gone!

Still, even without the bee, the window was fascinating. Standing up

on her back paws, Luna could poke
her head out of the window quite
easily. She'd spent a long time sitting
on Nadia's bedroom windowsill,
watching the cars and the people in
the street below, but this was much
more exciting. The world was just
out there for her to explore! She
could hear birds calling and someone
shouting in one of the yards. And
that delicious, strange breeze was
making her want to sniff and climb
and explore. It was definitely stronger
than it had been before.

Luna's ears twitched curiously at
a muffled bang from the bottom of
the stairs. She peered around over
her shoulder, but it was a noise she
didn't recognize. She didn't know that

it mattered, that the door
to the stairs had swung
shut behind her—the
air outside was much
more interesting.
Luna wriggled out
of the window
and stood
cautiously on
the very edge of
the frame.

She was on the roof!

"What's the matter?" Violet asked,
nudging Nadia's arm gently. They
were in art class, building fossils out
of papier mâché. Usually Nadia would

90

have been up to her elbows in sticky newspaper, but she'd hardly touched her side of the ammonite at all.

Nadia looked at Violet for a moment. She wasn't sure what her friend was going to think…. Then she sighed. "I just can't stop thinking about Luna and Gracie, that's all. No one seems to want to adopt Luna, and I don't understand why! But I'm actually really glad because I don't want her to go! Or Gracie either."

"Oh…." Violet nodded thoughtfully.

"I think your mom might take Gracie and Luna back to the rescue center soon, and give us another mother cat to foster," Nadia said in a small voice. She didn't want Violet to think she was criticizing her mom. "But … I wish we could just keep them...."

"You know, I bet my mom would be so happy to find a good home for Gracie if you wanted to keep them both," Violet said.

"I can't stop thinking about it!" Nadia gave her a hopeful look. "You really think she would be okay with it? My dad loves Gracie so much, too."

"Cats who've been wild for a long time are really hard to find homes for. My mom said the other day that she was a little worried about Gracie. It's like she's somewhere in between a feral cat who wants to live outside and a pet cat who wants to be with a family."

"But your mom said how hard it was to find people to foster mother cats, too." Nadia sighed. She'd been really proud that they were doing such a special job, and she felt guilty about giving it up, even if it meant that they got to keep Luna and Gracie. "She was so grateful to my mom, she said. We couldn't foster any more mothers if we had our own cats."

Violet nodded slowly. "That's true. But it sounds like Gracie has bonded with your dad—that's special. Mom should be throwing him a party!"

"It would be good to keep them together, too," Nadia said eagerly. "I think Luna really needs her mom. Even though we helped feed her, she and Gracie snuggle up together all the time, and Gracie's always washing Luna." She was silent for a minute, and then she gave Violet a determined look. "You've made me feel better about it. I'm going to talk to Mom and Dad tonight. I'm going to tell them that I think we have to keep Luna and Gracie. We just have to."

"I'd hug you if I wasn't covered in glue," Violet said, beaming at her.

Chapter Seven
Escape!

Luna edged carefully off of the window frame and onto the roof below, padding cautiously across the sloping surface. This was much more exciting to explore than the boxes under the bed. The clay tiles made it easy to grip, although they felt rough on her soft paws. Luna zigzagged up and down and stepped over onto a different part

of the roof. It seemed to turn a corner,
pointing farther out and away from the
bedroom window. But if she looked
around, she could still see the open
window behind her, ready to go back
whenever she wanted.

Another bee zoomed past, and she
hopped quickly after it and skidded
a little. It was only a tiny slip, but
Luna flattened down against the tiles
at once, clinging on as tightly as she
could. Her heart was thumping inside
her—that was close! She had to be
more careful.

It was getting colder, too, she
realized with a shiver. The bright
sun had disappeared, and the blue
of the sky was fading to a whitish-
gray. Luna twitched in surprise as a

raindrop splattered against the tiles next to her, and then another one, and then one on her nose. She clung to the roof, looking worriedly around as the rain splashed down. The reddish-brown tiles were darkening now, and the water was starting to run into the gutters. She huddled herself just under the roof ridge, the heavy rain plastering her fur flat against her body.

Luna let out a tiny meow—she didn't want to call too loudly, because she felt as if the slightest movement could make her paws slip again. Quietly, cautiously, she cried for her mother and for Nadia. She just wanted to go home….

At the school gates, Nadia hugged her dad tightly and waved good-bye to Violet. Violet grinned at her and gave her a thumbs up, wishing her luck.

"Why does it always start raining at school pick-up time?" Dad said, beckoning Nadia under his umbrella and rolling his eyes.

"Dad, I need to talk to you about something. It's important."

Dad gave her a worried look. "What's wrong? Has something happened?" He glanced back at the school. "Do I need to go and talk to Miss Evans?"

"No, it's about Luna. And Gracie." Nadia took a deep breath. "I think we should keep them."

Dad was silent for a moment. Then he sighed. "You know, I'm finding it hard to imagine my working day without Gracie lying on my desk. She even gave my hand a little headbutt today. First time she's done that. And I'd miss Luna trying to climb my legs so she can dance up and down on the keyboard."

Nadia squeezed his hand tight. "So … you think we should keep them, too?"

He smiled down
at Nadia. "Let's see
what your mom
says."

Nadia let go of
Dad's hand and
wrapped both of her
arms around his arm
instead, hugging it
tightly as they walked.
Dad loved Gracie and
Luna, too! They might, just
might, be able to keep them!

When they got home, Nadia dashed
upstairs to find Luna—it was what she
usually did right after school, but today

it seemed even more important. She wanted to tell Luna the news.

She hurried into her room, expecting to find Luna curled up on her comforter, or on the squishy cat bed she still shared with Gracie inside the closet. But there was no kitten waiting excitedly for her—and Gracie wasn't there, either.

"I hope Dad didn't leave his office door open again," Nadia muttered. The other day when he'd gone to get a cup of tea, Luna had added some very strange figures to a set of accounts he'd been working on.

Dad's office door was closed, though. Nadia stood in the hallway for a moment, feeling confused. Then she heard a worried-sounding meow from the end of the landing.

Gracie was standing by the door
to the stairs that led up to Mom and
Dad's room in the loft. As Nadia
watched, the cat stood up on her hind
paws and scratched anxiously at the
door. Then she looked around at Nadia
and meowed loudly.

"Did Luna get in
there?" Nadia asked
uncertainly. "But …
the door's closed."
Gracie
meowed again,
even louder,
and this time
her paws
thudded wildly
against the door.

"Okay...." Nadia reached out for the
door handle and Gracie backed up at
once, as though she understood that
she needed to be out of the way of the
opening door. As soon as Nadia pulled
it open, Gracie shot up the stairs, and
Nadia dashed after her.

"She isn't here, Gracie," Nadia said,
looking around her parents' room. "She
must be downstairs somewhere. Come
on. We'll go and look."

But Gracie wasn't listening. She
made a huge leap from the floor up
onto the shelving unit just under the
window. The *open* window!

"Oh! Gracie, no! You can't go
out there." Nadia flung herself after
Gracie, who was standing with her
front paws up against the window

frame, peering out at the roof.
Gracie didn't like to be touched, but
Nadia thought it would be worse
to let her out onto the roof than to
grab her. "You can't!" she gasped,
seizing Gracie just under her front
paws and pulling her back. She was
trying to be gentle, but Gracie was
so wriggly, desperately clinging on to
the window.

Then, from outside, there came a
tiny, frightened meow.

Gracie wriggled even harder and
Nadia stood on tiptoe, peering out of
the window. Out there on the roof
was a hunched, bedraggled ball of wet
fur.

"Luna!" Nadia breathed in horror.
She put Gracie on the bed and pulled

the window down a bit, so that the open gap was tiny. She was pretty sure Gracie couldn't squeeze out of that. Then she ran to the top of the loft stairs. "*Dad!* Luna's on the roof!" she yelled. "She's stuck! Help! Dad!" She could hear her dad thundering up the stairs.

"What? How did she even get up here?"

"I don't know!" Nadia wailed. "Come and see. Gracie was trying to get out, too. I had to shut the window."

Gracie was back up on the shelving unit now, pacing back and forth and meowing frantically. She looked as if she were desperate to get out of the window.

"That was smart," Dad said. He
pressed his nose against the glass,
trying to see out. "Oh, wow.... There
she is."

"I think she's stuck," Nadia said
worriedly.

"I don't see why she hasn't just
come back again," Dad said, frowning.
"Unless she got scared when it started

raining."

"What if she falls off?" Nadia whispered.

Dad put his arm around her. "I don't think she will. Don't worry. She's a good climber. Cats can get to the most incredible places sometimes." He sighed. "They just aren't always very good at getting back again."

Gracie meowed loudly again, staring at both of them, her eyes round with fear.

"We'll get her back," Nadia told the anxious cat. "We will, Dad, won't we?"

"Actually, I've got an idea," Dad said, hurrying to the stairs. "Don't let Gracie get out there, Nadia. I'll be back in a minute."

It felt much longer—Nadia kept pressing herself close to the window to check on the kitten. It had stopped raining, but Luna's fur was still plastered flat all over. She was usually so fluffy, but now she seemed scarily tiny.

At last she heard Dad coming back, muttering to himself and banging into things—and then he appeared at the top of the stairs with a long plank of wood. It was one of the pieces left over from building the deck in the yard, Nadia realized.

"What's that for?" Gracie was staring at him in horror, and Nadia thought maybe she was, too.

"It's a bridge," Dad said, trying to move around the bed to get the plank lined up with the window. "I think Luna's too scared to walk back around the corner of that wet roof. So if I rest this on the tiles, just next to her, she can go straight across instead."

"Oh...." Nadia smiled hopefully. "That's a great idea!"

"You need to stop Gracie from trying to get out of the window when I open it," Dad explained. "Actually, maybe we'd better put her downstairs."

Nadia looked at Gracie, and Gracie looked back. Every hair of her said that she wasn't going anywhere.

Dad sighed. "Maybe not. Okay. We're doing our best, you know," he muttered to Gracie. "Stay there." Carefully, he opened the window a little more and slid the piece of wood out. "I hope it's long enough…. Yes! There we go. Now we just have to hope Luna understands what she's supposed to do…."

Chapter Eight
Safe at Home

Luna gave a tiny meow of fright as the piece of wood came lumbering toward her out of the window. It clunked against the roof tiles, and she felt them shudder. What was happening? She could see Nadia's dad in the window, but she had no idea what he was trying to do, and she was too frightened to figure it out. She froze in place and closed her eyes tightly. Where was Nadia? Where was her mother? She was so cold and so scared, and so desperate to be home…. Everything seemed to be frozen. She couldn't make herself move, and she couldn't make herself think, either. She could only sit still, and wait, and hope.

"Is Luna coming?" Nadia demanded, squashing up close to Dad. It was hard to see around his shoulder with the shelving unit in the way.

"No…. Not yet," her dad said doubtfully. "I'm not sure she understands what we're trying to do—I thought she'd see it was a bridge, but

maybe it just looks like a big, scary
thing to her."

Nadia stood on tiptoe and then
caught her breath at the sight of Luna.
The piece of wood next to her made
her look even smaller. She had her eyes
closed, as though she were trying to
shut everything out.

"It's not working," she said, her voice going high and frightened. What if they couldn't get Luna back in? She didn't want to think about it, but she couldn't stop....

"I'm going to go and see if Pete's home next door. He has a ladder," Dad muttered. "I'll be back in a minute, Nadia. Don't let Gracie escape, okay? And don't lean out; it's not safe."

"All right," Nadia whispered. She wasn't absolutely sure she could stop Gracie, though. The window was only open enough for the wooden plank to fit through, but it was a fat piece of wood, and Gracie was a skinny cat.

Maybe we should let her try, Nadia thought, eyeing the anxious-looking tabby pacing the shelves. She'd seen

Gracie pick up her kittens in her mouth, although she hadn't done it in a little while. Was Luna too big to carry now? Nadia shuddered at the thought of Gracie walking back along that plank bridge, with Luna dangling from her mouth. No, that was *not* a good idea.

Nadia looked out at Luna again. The orange kitten's fur was still wet enough to be autumn-leaf dark, and Nadia was pretty sure that she was shivering. They had to do something soon....

Gracie couldn't carry Luna back.... But maybe she and Nadia together could persuade Luna to try for herself.

"Look...." Nadia tapped at the window frame, and Gracie gave her an alert, anxious glance. "She's out there.

We have to get her back in here. We have to get her home. Come on, Gracie. Call her," she pleaded. "I wish I could make you understand." She looked out again. "Oh, her eyes are open!"

Luna looked a tiny bit less like a statue kitten—she was staring at the window now.

"Oh, ow!" Nadia squeaked as Gracie clawed her way up beside her, scratching at the edge of the window and practically hanging from her front paws. Gracie meowed loudly, and Nadia saw Luna's ears flicker. She'd *definitely* heard that.

"Yes, yes, Luna, come on…," she called—not too loud, because she didn't want to scare her. Very slowly, Luna eased out of her terrified crouch, wobbling on to her little white paws and eyeing them nervously.

Gracie meowed again, and wriggled, and Nadia had to grab her. She really didn't want two cats out on the roof. In the panic, the two of them almost missed Luna stepping cautiously onto the plank of wood.

Luna could see them both, her mother and Nadia calling to her. They sounded scared, and that frightened Luna—but it made her want to be back with them more. Nadia was home. Nadia had fed her and cared for her; she made Luna think of curling up asleep together, of gentle pets and delicious food and all

117

those bottles of milk....

They were right there, only a short distance away. The plank of wood actually looked wide and flat now, very safe. She stood up shakily and set her paw onto the fragile bridge. It didn't give at all, and the tiny kitten started to pad across. She could see the blur of a striped face and Nadia's dark, worried eyes ahead.

"You're doing it! Great job, Luna! I'll open the window a little more." There was a scuffle, and Luna saw her mother's white whiskers flutter as she suddenly disappeared from the open crack of window. Then she froze,

huddling down against the plank as
the window creaked opened wider. Her
bridge shook a little, but she saw Nadia
again and heard her call softly, "It's all
right! Come on, you can get all the way
in now. Come on, Luna…."

The kitten paced daintily to the
edge of the window. She hesitated at
the end of the wooden plank, unsure
about the drop down, but then she felt
Nadia's hands close gently around her.
She was lifted and immediately tucked
close against Nadia's T-shirt. She could
feel her hands shaking.

"Nadia, you've got her!"

Nadia looked up in surprise to see

her mom at the bedroom door. She was
sitting on the edge of her mom and
dad's bed, with Luna cuddled against
her and Gracie standing half on her lap,
nosing against her fingers. Slowly, she
put Luna down on the bedcover so that
Gracie could sniff her over.

"I didn't know you were home," Nadia
said, standing up to hug her mom.

"I just got back from work—I met
your dad coming from Pete's with a
ladder. Oh! Wait a minute." She went
to the window and called, "Rafi! It's all
right; Nadia's got her. Put that ladder
down!" Then she glanced at Gracie
and Luna. "Should we take them
downstairs? I want to get them away
from that window. It worked, then?" she
added as Nadia picked up Luna, and

Gracie followed them down the stairs.

"Gracie and I called her," Nadia explained. "Oh, Mom, I was so scared that she was going to fall off of the roof."

Mom shivered. "When your dad told me what had happened, I had a horrible feeling that I was going to get up here and find you out on the roof with her. Let's go into your room. I think it's where Gracie and Luna both feel safest. We can get a towel to dry her off, too. She's soaked."

Nadia sat down on her bed, and Gracie leaped up beside her to nuzzle at Luna. Her own mom was doing the same thing, Nadia realized, smiling a little as Mom sat down on the bed, too, and put an arm around her and helped her to rub Luna dry.

After a while, Luna wriggled out of the towel and sat in the middle of the comforter with her eyes closed, while Gracie licked her ears thoroughly. Luna looked as though she wasn't happy about it, but she knew it wouldn't be a good idea to try and run away.

"Pete took the ladder back," Nadia's dad said as he came into the room and collapsed on the beanbag chair. "I have to admit, I'm glad I didn't have to climb up it, even with him holding on to it for me. It looked a little shaky."

"I don't want any of you up ladders, or wandering around roofs," Nadia's mom said with a shudder, watching Luna hunch up as Gracie continued washing her. "I'm so glad you got her back safely, Nadia. I couldn't bear it if anything had happened to her. It made me think—it's going to be so hard to say good-bye." She looked over at Nadia's dad and sighed.

"What if we kept her, Mom?" Nadia burst out. "Kept both of them? They love each other so much. It was Gracie who knew where Luna was. She was scratching at the door to the stairs."

"Definitely both of them," Dad said. "I know you had to persuade me about the fostering when we started, Farida, but I don't want to give them back now, either." He leaned over and stretched out his hand to Gracie. The tabby cat eyed him for a moment, and then she stopped licking Luna and licked Dad's hand instead. Luna grabbed her chance, scooting away to climb into Nadia's lap.

Mom laughed. "I never expected your dad would fall in love with a cat, Nadia. I was definitely right about you, though...."

Nadia looked between them anxiously. "So ... Mom ... can we?"

"Yes." Mom reached out to rub Luna's damp ears. "Yes, let's keep

them. I know Violet's mom hoped
we might foster another mom about
to have kittens, but actually we might
have found her another foster home
instead. Your nani said she was going
to call Violet's mom. She misses
Milo so much, but she's not ready for
another cat of her own just yet, and
she'd like to try fostering."

"Nani would be perfect!" Nadia said,
nodding eagerly.

"You know what we are?" Mom said,
shaking her head. "Violet's mom told
me that there's a name for it. Foster
fail. That's when you're only supposed
to be fostering a pet for a few weeks
and you end up keeping it."

Dad shook his head. "I don't think
we failed! These two are going to have

a forever home, aren't they? A home with people who already love them."

"Forever, Luna. Did you hear that?" Nadia whispered to the kitten as she stomped her paws up and down and then collapsed into a sleepy ball on Nadia's legs.

Luna let out a soft, wheezy kitten snore. Or maybe a purr. Forever was good.